JASPER & SCRUFF

THE CAFÉ COMPETITION

*For my very
supportive parents
and husband,
Gavin*

tiger tales

5 River Road, Suite 128, Wilton, CT 06897

Published in the United States 2022
Originally published in Great Britain 2021
by the Little Tiger Group

Text and illustrations copyright © 2021 Nicola Colton
ISBN-13: 978-1-6643-4012-1
ISBN-10: 1-6643-4012-2

Printed in China
STP/1800/0415/0821
All rights reserved
2 4 6 8 10 9 7 5 3 1

www.tigertalesbooks.com

MIX
Paper from
responsible sources
FSC® C020056

The Forest Stewardship Council®
(FSC®) is a global, not-for-profit
organization dedicated to the
promotion of responsible forest
management worldwide. FSC®
defines standards based on agreed
principles for responsible forest
stewardship that are supported
by environmental, social, and
economic stakeholders.
To learn more, visit www.fsc.org

by Nicola Colton

JASPER
& SCRUFF

THE CAFÉ
COMPETITION

tiger tales

J asper was the type of cat who liked to cook fancy food and visit fancy restaurants.

Scruff was the type of puppy who liked to eat. Salted caramel was his favorite. He liked nothing better than Salted Caramel Cake washed down with a salted caramel milkshake.

So they listened to their tummies
and opened a café of their own.
They served Scruff's favorite cake,
of course, but there was one specialty
that their café soon became known for....

With Scruff's nose for flavor and
Jasper's eye for detail, they came up
with the perfect sandwich. Customers
traveled from far and wide to give
the Cheese Monsieur a try.

One day, Jasper and Scruff were in the kitchen preparing sandwiches.

Jasper was stirring a large pot of cheese sauce. It was what made their Cheese Monsieur so delicious. He checked the recipe and added a pinch of smoked paprika.

"Pass me the Sparkling Catnip Juice, Scruff," said Jasper. "Scruff?"

Jasper turned around. Scruff was
spinning plates like he was in the
circus. He had asked Scruff to dry
the plates, but not like that!

"Scruff!"
yelled Jasper at the top of his voice.

Startled, Scruff began to sway. Jasper's
eyes grew as large as saucers as he
watched the plates spin toward him.

"Ow!" yelped Jasper as one hit him
between the eyes. The rest
crashed to the floor.

"Oh, I'm sorry!" panted Scruff.
"I was just trying out a new way
of drying the plates."

"You should stick to dish towels."
Jasper rubbed the bump on his
forehead. "Now can you PLEASE
pass me the Catnip Juice?"

"Sure," said Scruff, standing on tiptoe
to reach it. "Why do we add this stuff
anyway? Catnip is yucky!"

"Well, you could have fooled me, Scruff. You ate five Cheese Monsieurs yesterday! The catnip gives our sauce its signature tang, and the bubbles make it extra-rich. It's my secret ingredient!"

"Ah, so that's why it's not written down in the recipe!" said Scruff, glancing over at Jasper's personal cookbook.

"Now make yourself useful and stir this sauce." Jasper adjusted his chef's hat. "It's almost lunchtime—our busiest time of day. I'm going to check and see if Milly and Milo need some help waiting tables."

11

But Jasper was met with a surprising
sight. The café was empty—except
for Milly and Milo dancing away
by the jukebox.

"Hey!" said Milly as she pirouetted
on her skates. "It's so quiet today that we
thought we'd spend some time dancing."

"Salty Cyril came by earlier for his Seaweed Shake and an extra-salty slice of caramel cake," Milo put in. "But he's been the only customer all morning."

"Hmm, that's odd," said Jasper.

"Where is everyone?" called Scruff,
poking his head through the service
hatch. "What's going on?"

"I don't know," said Jasper. He went
to look through the window.
"I can see a big crowd outside.
Let's investigate. Milo, keep an eye
on the sauce, will you?"

Across the street, a red carpet had
been rolled out. Cameras flashed,
and the crowd cheered.

Jasper and Scruff hurried to see what was going on. But their view was blocked by two large rhinos.

"Oh, we'll never see anything from here," groaned Jasper.

"I'll climb up on your shoulders," said Scruff.

"Wow, that's some crowd!" said Scruff.

"We know that already," sighed Jasper.
"What else can you see?"

"There's a ribbon wrapped around the building across the street. Oh, and Ms. Merry the mayor is there!"

"Then it must be something important," said Jasper.

"It's a new restaurant, I think." Craning his neck, Scruff spotted a sign above the door. "The Sophisticafé!" he gasped. "You don't think this has anything to do with—"

"The Sophisticats!" interrupted Jasper, pointing to a large limo. Lady Catterly stepped out, and the crowd *oohed* as she walked up the red carpet.

"But I don't see Reginald or Oswald anywhere," said Scruff, scanning the crowd.

The mayor held out a huge pair of
scissors and cut the ribbon.

"I declare the Sophisticafé
officially open!" she announced.

"Yes, welcome everyone," Lady Catterly crooned into the microphone. "As head chef, I think you are all going to love our signature dish!"

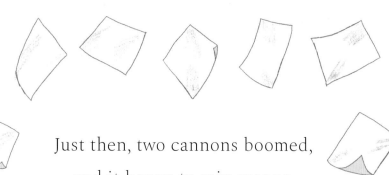

Just then, two cannons boomed,
and it began to rain menus.
Scruff leapt up and caught
one between his teeth. He
passed it to Jasper.

Holding it by a corner with
his hanky to avoid the drool,
Jasper began to read.

Sophisticafé

Le Menu

Appetizers

Truffle Tarts

Side Dish

Pawpaw & Catmint Salad

Signature Dish

To be revealed at launch dinner tonight

Dessert

Cinnamon Swirl Cake

"What do you think their signature
dish is going to be?" said Scruff.

"I'm not sure," said Jasper. "Let's see if
we can find out."

Jasper and Scruff marched toward
the café doors. But as they reached
the front of the line, they hit a solid
wall of fur. Two enormous gorillas
stood behind a velvet rope.

"Invitation, please." The nearest gorilla held out his hand.

"I don't have one," said Jasper.
"I just want to take a quick look inside."

"Invitation only," grunted the other gorilla, pushing the pair to one side.

"Hi, Jasper and Scruff!" said a cheery
voice. They looked around to see
famous ballet dancer Bunny Moloko.
She was arm in arm with Alvis
Pawsley, Jasper's favorite singer.

"Aren't you going in?" asked Alvis.

"We're not invited," said Scruff,
looking down.

"Oh, I thought the whole town was,"
said Bunny.

"We don't want to eat at that copycat
café anyway," said Jasper, turning tail.
"Come on, Scruff!"

Back at their café, they were met with a sorry sight. Milly and Milo were covered in sticky goo.

"I don't know what happened," said Milly. "We had this really demanding customer—"

"First he wanted us to wipe his table.
Then he couldn't find the song he
wanted on the jukebox. And when we
got back to the kitchen, the sauce had
exploded!" Milo finished.

Jasper and Scruff rushed into the kitchen, and Jasper let out a deep groan. The walls were covered from floor to ceiling in cheese sauce.

"How did the sauce explode?" said Scruff. "It's never done that before!"

"And I don't remember leaving the window open," said Jasper, twiddling his whiskers thoughtfully.

As Jasper started to wipe down the counter, he noticed that his personal cookbook was in the wrong place. And a page had been torn out.

"My Cheese Monsieur recipe! It's gone!" he gasped. "This looks like the work of the Sophisticats."

Scruff nodded. "It's not the first time they've tried to trick us. It's lucky you didn't write down your secret ingredient."

"I guess," said Jasper with a sigh. "Well, we'll just have to finish cleaning up and close for today. It's not like we have any customers anyway."

"Leave the cleaning to me!" said Scruff.

"What are you—?" Jasper began as Scruff started to lick the sauce from the floor.

"We can't let all of this delicious sauce go to waste!" yapped Scruff.

Just as Jasper changed the sign
from open to closed, Zach came
to the door.

"I'm sorry, Zach," said Jasper.
"You'll have to come back tomorrow."

"What a shame," said Zach. "I much
prefer it here to the Sophisticafé.
Their staff is very rude."

Suddenly, Jasper had an idea. "I'm sure
we can whip up a milkshake. Have a
seat. Oh, and I don't suppose you still
have your invitation, do you?"

That evening, a disguised Jasper and Scruff joined the line outside the Sophisticafé.

When they finally reached the front, Jasper pulled Zach's invitation from his coat pocket.

"Let's hope this works," said Jasper, giving his mustache a twirl.

Jasper waved the invitation at the gorillas.

"Phew!" said Scruff as one of them raised the velvet rope.

A surly waiter showed them
to their table.

"Wow! It IS fancy in here," said Jasper.
Everything from the chandeliers to the
fountain to the grand piano sparkled.

"Let's hope the food is good," said
Scruff. "I'm starving!"

"We're hoping it's bad, remember?"
said Jasper. "Besides, aren't you full
after gobbling all of that cheese sauce?"

"I can always eat!" said Scruff.

Jasper picked up a menu. "Just as I
thought," he hissed. "The Sophisticats
have stolen our—"

"Quick, hide!" whispered Scruff as
Lady Catterly swished past in
a bejeweled chef's hat and
glittering pants.

She stopped at a table to schmooze
with a local TV news reporter.

"Ahem!" coughed the waiter,
appearing behind Jasper.
"Can I take your order, sir?"

"I think I'll have your signature dish—
the Sophisticheese," said Jasper,
lowering his menu.

"Me, too!" said Scruff.

"At last!" said Scruff when
the waiter returned.

But his tail drooped when the food
was put in front of him—a very small
sandwich on a very large plate.

"Is that it?" Scruff's tummy groaned
as he looked around the restaurant.
Everyone was eating tiny sandwiches
with knives and forks.

"This all seems a bit much
for a sandwich!" muttered Jasper,
picking at the gold flake garnish.

Scruff grabbed a long fork with two prongs.

"I think you'll find that's a pickle fork.
It's quite unsuitable for sandwiches,"
said the waiter, looking down his nose.

But Scruff was too hungry for silly
rules. He leaned over his sandwich
and gobbled it up in one bite.

"How was it?" asked Jasper. "Scruff?"

Scruff was clutching his throat.

"Ack!"

Scruff coughed up a golden ball of sandwich. It flew out of his mouth, taking his mustache with it.

Smash! The ball crashed into a tray
of crystal glasses. Then... *Splash!*
It bounced into a bowl of soup,
dousing a family of well-dressed pugs.

The music stopped. Everyone fell
silent and turned to look at
Jasper and Scruff.

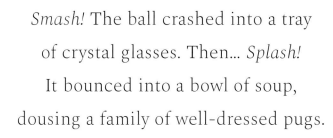

"You two!" screeched Lady Catterly.
"You were not invited, you fraudulent
furballs! Security! Take care of
this riffraff!"

Jasper and Scruff felt rough, hairy
hands pick them up. A moment later,
they found themselves back on the
other side of the velvet rope.

Just then, they heard a *click-clacking* sound. Jasper looked up.

"It's Gaspard le Skunk!" he whispered as a skunk in shiny shoes and a velvet jacket strode up the red carpet and into the Sophisticafé. He was clutching a leather-bound notebook with three golden paws embossed on the front.

"Never heard of him," said Scruff.

"Really?" said Jasper.
"He's a famous food critic. Only the
world's finest restaurants are awarded
his three-paw rating."

The pair watched as Gaspard was
seated at the window.

"Speaking of food, I'm still hungry,"
said Scruff. "Let's go home for a snack."

"No, wait," said Jasper. "I need to see what
he thinks of the Sophisticheese."

Before long, Gaspard's sandwich arrived.
He picked up the plate and examined it
from every angle. His tail swished from
side to side as he gave it a sniff.

Then, picking up a large ornate fork,
he prodded the sandwich. He nibbled
a corner and scribbled something
in his notebook.

"Pffffft!" said Scruff. "There was hardly enough sandwich for a fork! Can we go now?"

"Shhh," said Jasper as Lady Catterly clapped her hands, and a dessert cart was wheeled over.

Scruff licked his lips.
"Mmmm, that's a lot of cake!"

"Gaspard has a sweet tooth,"
said Jasper. "Oh, look!"

Gaspard studied the cart, sniffed,
and then shook his tail. Jasper's face
lit up as the skunk got to his feet.

"What is it?" asked Scruff.

"Remember the menu?" said Jasper,
and Scruff nodded.

"All of the cakes have cinnamon in them,
and Gaspard doesn't like cinnamon. His
taste buds are so sensitive that he can't
stand even the merest hint of spice or
excess seasoning. They're lucky that he
didn't make a stink. Gaspard has a way
of letting you know when his taste buds
aren't happy."

Jasper straightened his bow tie as the restaurant door swung open and Gaspard stepped out. "Unlike the Sophisticats, I happen to know what his favorite cake is! We have to get him to review our café."

The next morning, Jasper sat in a
booth busily redesigning the menu.

Scruff leaned over his shoulder
and read aloud.

"What is this, Jasper?
Our regulars love the Cheese
Monsieur and Salted Caramel Cake.
This all sounds very complicated."

Menu

Lobster Parfait
{ with crouton jewels }

Artichoke Fricassee

Opera Cake
{ with candied rose petals }

"Oh, Scruff!" Jasper rolled his eyes. "We have to think big. Gaspard won't want a boring sandwich or an ordinary cake when he comes this evening. Complicated is what will win us our three-paw rating!"

"But Jasper, we created the sandwich and cake together. Everyone loves them!"

"Gaspard isn't just anyone," said Jasper.
"Now, I need to start baking. Can you
put these new menus out and update
the menu board? Oh, and Scruff,
remember to increase the prices."

Regular customers came all morning, but when they saw the new menu and the new prices, they left right away.

Jasper was too busy in the kitchen to notice.

"I think we should give Milly and Milo the evening off," said Scruff through the hatch. "We've had no customers all day."

"Yes, good idea," muttered Jasper, glancing up from the saucepan of glaze.

"Jasper, are you listening?" said Scruff. "We lost all of our customers today."

"Don't worry about that," said Jasper. "The café will be packed when we get our three-paw rating. Has my delivery arrived yet? It's almost six. Gaspard will be here soon. I'm still waiting for some special ingredients I ordered. And the sparkler for the top of the cake."

Ting-a-ling!

"That must be it now," said Jasper.

"Package for a Mr. Jasper," said a black cat, poking his head through the front door.

"Hello! I can sign for it," said Scruff.

There's something familiar about that cat,
he thought as he reached for the box.
But the cat's cap was pulled down so low
that Scruff could only see his whiskers.

Jasper was just finishing unpacking the
box when the town clock struck six.

Bong! Bong! Bong! Bong! Bong! Bong!

"Gaspard will be here any second!"
he panicked. "You'll have to greet him
at the door, Scruff. Now where's that
sweet paprika for the appetizer?"

Ting-a-ling!

"Ah, so this is Paws Café," said Gaspard, scowling down at Scruff.

"Welcome, Mr. Skunk," said Scruff. "Would you like the booth by the jukebox? It's the best seat in the house. You can play any music you'd like!"

"How quaint," said Gaspard.
"Aren't you going to take my jacket?"

"Sure, if you want me to," said Scruff,
scratching his ear. Gaspard marked
an X in his notebook.

Scruff gulped. They weren't
off to a good start.

Gaspard looked at the menu
and brightened.

"Lobster Parfait, Artichoke Fricassee,
and Opera Cake. My favorites! This
place might be better than it looks."

"I'll bring the first dish right away,"
said Scruff.

Scruff placed the Lobster Parfait and
a glass of Sparkling Catnip Juice in
front of Gaspard while Jasper looked
on nervously through the hatch.

Gaspard took a forkful and then
another. He smiled and made a
note in his book.

But then his tail started to twitch.

"H-h-h-hot! My throat!
It's burning!" he cried.

Scruff ran to the kitchen for a jug of water.

Gaspard gulped it down.

"The menu didn't say it would be ... spicy,"
he wheezed.

"It's not meant to be," said Scruff,
frowning. "How about some
Artichoke Fricassee?"

Scruff brought out the next dish.
Gaspard sniffed, and then carefully
tasted a mouthful.

The skunk's tail shuddered.
"Yuck! This is as salty as the sea!
Take it back!"

That's funny, thought Scruff. *Why
would Jasper add too much salt?*

"Well, I'm sure you'll love our
Opera Cake!" he said.

As Scruff brought out the cake,
Gaspard smiled.

"Excellent mirror glaze and a nice touch
with the sparkler. You may surprise me
yet," he said, his tail swishing happily.

Jasper looked on with crossed paws.

Just as Gaspard was about to nibble
on a rose petal, there was a blinding
flash of light.

Covered in chocolate goo, Gaspard's tail
flicked furiously from side to side.

"This really takes the cake! I've tasted enough. Ask the chef to come out here. Now!" He wiped ganache from his brow.

Jasper slunk out.

"This is the WORST meal I've ever had! There's only one rating I can give this place." Gaspard lifted his tail.

"Scruff! Get down!" said Jasper, pulling him under a table.

Gaspard released the most terrible stench
before *click-clacking* out of the door.

Jasper and Scruff crawled
into the kitchen to escape the
eye-watering smell.

"The special ingredients...," muttered Jasper, spotting the box on the counter. "Pass me the sweet paprika, Scruff."

Jasper tasted a pinch and started to cough. "It's extra h-h-hot chili powder!" he spluttered.

"Look!" said Scruff, removing a slip of paper from the bottom of the box.

On it were printed the words:

> We hope your evening ends with a bang!
>
> from the Sophisticats

Holding their noses, Jasper and Scruff hurried through the café and flung open the door. Across the street, Lady Catterly, Reginald, and Oswald were bent over with laughter. Reginald was still wearing a delivery uniform but had taken off his cap.

"I knew I recognized those whiskers!"
said Scruff.

"We've lost our customers, and it's all
been for nothing!" said Jasper,
his head in his paws.

"Don't worry," said Scruff. "We'll get things back to the way they were. Our regular customers will return. You'll see."

A few days later, once the fumes had cleared, the café was packed again.

"I be 'appy to see the ole menu again," said Salty Sid. "This be me favorite cake!"

"And I love the Cheese Monsieur,"
said Zach from a nearby table.

"These are the only reviews I care
about," said Jasper as he squirted some
extra whipped cream on Sid's shake.

"That's good," said Bunny Moloko, popping up from behind a newspaper. "Because there's not a very good write-up in the paper today, I'm afraid."

Jasper sighed. "I didn't expect a dazzling review."

"It looks like the Sophisticafé only got a two-paw rating, though," Alvis added. "Gaspard said that their signature dish, the Sophisticheese, was missing a certain something."

"Two paws? Lady Catterly won't be happy about that," said Jasper.

"She's not!" said Scruff. "Look out the window!"

Lady Catterly was jumping up and down on a newspaper. "Two paws? Two paws?" she yowled. "This is the finest café in town!"

"She looks pretty upset!" said Jasper.

"We actually have a question for you,"
said Bunny. "We were wondering if
you could cater our wedding."
She held up her paw to show
a shiny engagement ring.

"We're getting married next Saturday,"
added Alvis. "We love the food here.
And you even have a jukebox!"

The following Saturday, Paws Café played host to the glitziest event in town—Alvis and Bunny's wedding.

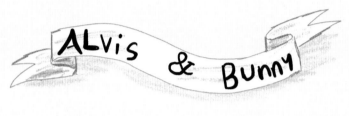

Jasper and Scruff made Cheese Monsieurs for all of the guests, and a huge salted caramel wedding cake. The music played long into the night.

The whole town had been invited, except for three snooty cats.

"I'm glad we're sticking to what works," said Scruff.

"Yes. I'm sorry for getting carried away," said Jasper. "The only paw rating I care about is this one." Smiling, he high-fived his best friend.